Animaniacs Adventures

ISBN 0-590-53528-5

12 11 10 9 8 7 6 5 4 3 2 1   5 6 7 8 9/9 0/0

Printed in the U.S.A.   23

First Scholastic printing, November 1995

Designed by Alfred Giuliani

Animaniacs Adventures

Two Wacky Tales in One Cool Book!

Adapted by Jane B. Mason
Based upon television scripts by Peter Hastings,
Paul Rugg, Earl Kress and Tom Ruegger

Illustrated by John Costanza
Cover illustration by Allen Helbig

SCHOLASTIC INC.
New York Toronto London Auckland Sydney

Chalkboard Bungle

It was a busy day at the big Hollywood movie studio. Cars sped in and out of the parking lot, bearing important visitors.

In one of the cars was a woman on a mission. Miss Hortense Flameel's car screeched to a halt in front of the guard shack.

Ralph the security guard stepped out. "Uh, may I help you?" he asked.

"I'm the new studio teacher," Miss Flameel said.

Ralph scratched his head. "Duh, you must be new here. I ain't never seen you before."

Miss Flameel raised an eyebrow in disgust. "*Ain't never?*" she repeated. "That's a double negative. I'm going to have to give you an *F*!" She reached into her blouse pocket and pulled out a red

4

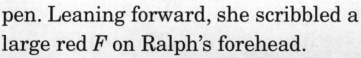

pen. Leaning forward, she scribbled a large red *F* on Ralph's forehead.

Ralph shook his head as she sped toward the office of Mr. T. Plotz, the big studio boss. "My folks are gonna kill me," he groaned.

A few minutes later, Miss Flameel was in a meeting with the chief executive officer, Mr. T. Plotz.

"Your assignment will not be easy," Plotz told her. He paused to pop a piece of gum into his mouth. "The Animaniacs are not normal—"

"I will not tolerate gum chewing," Miss Flameel snapped. "Come, come. Give me the gum." She smacked the back of his head. The gum flew into her hand. She pulled out her red pen and scrawled a big *F* across Mr. Plotz's forehead.

Mr. Plotz couldn't believe it! His face turned red. He pounded his fist on the desk.

"Do you mind?" he shouted. "I am not in class. I hired you!"

Miss Flameel raised an eyebrow. But she didn't say anything.

"It's your job to get those zany Animaniacs under control!"

A crooked smile crossed Miss Flameel's face. "There hasn't been a child yet that I haven't been able to control. When do I get to meet the dear little ones?"

That afternoon, Ralph delivered a crate to Miss Flameel's classroom. The crate was clearly marked with a warning: DANGER — VOLATILE CONTENTS! but she paid no attention.

"Duh, these is your students," Ralph said nervously. He handed her a crowbar and dashed for the door.

Miss Flameel pried open the crate. Out popped Yakko, Wakko, and Dot — better known as the Animaniacs. Before she had a chance to call the class to order, they broke into a wild song and dance.

"School, school, school," they sang in unison. "Our first day of school. We're eager little learners. So fill our heads with lotsa facts...."

They dashed around the room, then stacked Miss Flameel's arms with books ...until she was completely buried! "This is a classroom, not a music hall!" Miss Flameel shouted from behind the wall of books. "Now find your seats.

"We will begin by reciting the Pledge of Allegiance."

She put her hand over her heart. The Animaniacs turned to face the flag.

"Please repeat after me," Miss Flameel instructed.

The Animaniacs stared at the flag. "Please repeat after me," they echoed.

"No. No. No," Miss Flameel said. "Wait until I start, then repeat after me."

"No. No. No," the Animaniacs said, their faces serious. "Wait until I start, then repeat after me."

Miss Flameel tried to get the Animaniacs to say the Pledge of Allegiance, but they would only repeat after her.

"That's it!" she finally screamed, running from the room.

"That's it!" The Animaniacs ran screaming from the room, too. A moment later Yakko, Wakko, and Dot ran back in.

Turning to the flag, they put their hands over their hearts.

"With liberty and justice for all," they ended proudly.

Later that afternoon, the Animaniacs were back in class.

"Do you want to see our homework?" Yakko asked.

Miss Flameel stretched out her hand.

"You can't see it. Our dog ate it," Yakko said.

"Grrrr!" Wakko had turned into a dog. He chomped on their homework.

Miss Flameel grabbed the paper. "Bad dog!" she hollered. "Give me that!" She pulled. And pulled. And pulled some more. Wakko bared his teeth. He wasn't letting go.

"Give it now!" Miss Flameel shouted.

Wakko opened his mouth, let go of the papers, and sent Miss Flameel flying!

Miss Flameel crashed into the blackboard. A heap of wooden blocks fell on top of her.

She scowled at the Animaniacs through the fallen blocks. "Yakko, can you count to one hundred?" she said.

Yakko grinned. "One, two," he began, "skip a few, ninety-nine, one hundred."

Miss Flameel sighed and shook her head. "Let's move on to science," she said. "Dot, what can you tell me about the great scientists of the eighteenth century?"

"They're all dead."

"No, no, no," Miss Flameel said.

"All right," Dot agreed. "They're all living."

"No, no, no," Miss Flameel said again. She reached into her blouse and pulled out an oxygen mask. She breathed deeply in an attempt to calm down!

"Let's try grammar," the teacher said a few minutes later. She walked over to the blackboard.

"The dog ran in the rain," Miss Flameel said as she wrote the sentence on the board.

Behind her, Yakko, Wakko, and Dot whacked a plastic cone back and forth. They were playing badminton!

"*Dog* is the subject. *Ran* is the verb." Miss Flameel turned around. But the Animaniacs were fast. They dashed to their seats.

The teacher turned back to the board. "Now the verb ..." she began.

But the Animaniacs were too busy hopping on pogo sticks to pay attention.

" ... could be conjugated so that —" She turned around quickly. But before she could catch them in the act, the Animaniacs were sitting quietly in their seats. "I know what you're doing," she said slyly. "I have eyes in the back of my head."

"Really?" Yakko said excitedly. "So do we!"

The Animaniacs turned around to show eyes in the back of their heads . . . and they blinked!

Miss Flameel glared at her students. "It's time for a pop quiz!" she threatened.

"Pop quiz!" Dot exclaimed happily. She jumped up, blindfolded Yakko, and set two cans of soda pop on the table.

Yakko took a sip of Fizolla and smacked his lips. Then he tasted Burpola and did the same thing. "I like the first one!" he declared.

Miss Flameel jumped up and down in a rage. "Stop that!" she screeched. "Sit at your desks this instant!"

The three kids scrambled to their seats, but Miss Flameel had had enough. She pulled out her red pen once again. A second later, she wrote a big *F* on Yakko's forehead.

"Hey, you can't do that to him!" Dot exclaimed.

Soon Dot had an *F* on her forehead, too.

But when Miss Flameel put an *F* on Wakko's forehead, she had gone too far.

His face turned red. He began to shake. *Kaboom!* He blasted off like a rocket, slamming right into Miss Flameel!

Wakko snatched her red pen and scrawled a huge *F* on the teacher's forehead. Then he sat back and sighed. "I feel better," he said.

Later that day, Ralph the security guard entered the classroom.

"You done with the Warner Brothers?" he asked.

Miss Flameel turned from the blackboard. "Yes," she replied. "Take them away."

Ralph dragged the crate out the door. As it closed behind him, Miss Flameel smiled. Then she pulled off a mask. That was no Miss Flameel! That was Dot! Yakko and Wakko popped out from under the dress.

"Recess!" Yakko crowed.

Outside, a crate was being lifted up to the water tower.

"Get me out of here *right now*!" a voice screeched from inside. "I'll give you an *F*! Do you hear me? *F!F!F!*"

Wacky Tale #2

The Taming of the Screwy

In the Hollywood movie studio, Mr. T. Plotz, chief executive officer and big boss, was meeting with Dr. Scratchansniff.

"Money!" Mr. Plotz was saying. "We need more money! I've invited some powerful investors here, and they're prepared to give us <u>one billion dollars</u>!"

"That's a one with *lots* of zeros after it," the doctor said, amazed.

Mr. Plotz walked over to the window. "Tomorrow is the most important day in the studio's history," he declared. "I'm throwing a big party. Every star in Hollywood will be here. The investors will get the royal treatment and *we'll* get the check.

"There's just one catch," he went on.
"Before they invest, they want to meet
everyone who works here . . .

" … including the Animaniacs."

Dr. Scratchansniff turned pale. "No!" he exclaimed. "Don't let the investors meet the Animaniacs. They're out of control! They're koo-koo! They're —"

"Your responsibility!" the chairman finished. "You are the studio psychiatrist."

Dr. Scratchansniff frowned. As much as he wanted to deny it, it was true.

"You have twenty-four hours to teach them some manners," Mr. Plotz said. "I can't have those . . . those . . ." A look of confusion crossed his face. "What are they?" he asked.

The doctor sighed. "I don't know," he admitted.

"Well, whatever they are, I can't have them ruin this party," the chairman finished.

"All right. I'll try to control them, " the doctor said.

"That's not good enough," T. Plotz said. "Do it!"

Later that day, Ralph the security guard brought a large wooden crate into Scratchansniff's office. It was marked THIS END UP, but the arrows went in all four directions! Ralph handed the doctor a crowbar and dashed out of the room.

Dr. Scratchansniff pried open the crate. "Mmmm...mmm...oof!" He strained with the effort.

The lid popped open, and the three Animaniacs leaped out. "Hello, Doctor Scratchansniff," they all said at once. Before the doctor could say a word, they broke into song. They raced all over the room, belting out line after line.

"Stop that! Stop!" Dr. Scratchansniff shouted. "Be quiet, please! I have something to tell you!"

"Ooo, story time!" Yakko said.

"Cut to the scary part," said Wakko.

"What scary part?" the doctor asked.

"The part with my pet!" Dot explained, pulling out her pet box.

"Raaaaar!" A ferocious monster popped out of the box!

Startled, Scratchansniff fell back onto his chair. "Now listen," he said breathlessly. "The studio is giving a big, fancy party for some new investors, with movie stars and everything."

"Movie stars!" the Animaniacs exclaimed.

"Michelle Pfeiffer," Yakko said dreamily. Yakko always dreamed about that beautiful actress.

"Mel Gibson," Dot added with a sigh. She was *crazy* over Mel.

"Don Knotts!" Wakko finished excitedly. They all turned to stare at him.

Scratchansniff cleared his throat. "But you can only go if I train you to be polite, clean, well-dressed children on your best behavior."

The Animaniacs' smiles turned into pouts.

"I thought you said it was a party," Dot complained.

"Yes or no?" the doctor asked.

The Animaniacs huddled. "Buzz, buzz, buzz, walla, walla," they murmured. Then they buzzed some more.

"*Yes* or *no*?" the doctor repeated nervously. His career was at stake.

Yakko smiled. "Doc, you've got yourself a deal!"

A little later, Dr. Scratchansniff and the nurse began a lesson on etiquette. "We'll start with the receiving line," he said.

Before Scratchansniff could blink, the Animaniacs had formed a conga line. "One, two, three, kick! One, two, three —"

"That's a <u>conga</u> line!" the doctor exclaimed.

"Nice to know you're up on your dance steps," Yakko said approvingly.

The doctor rubbed his hands on his face in frustration. "Now, in a receiving line, a proper greeting is 'How dooo you dooo?' Why don't you try it, Yakko?"

Yakko stepped forward, gave a little bow, and shook the nurse's hand.

"How dooo you dooo?" he asked. Then he hopped into her arms and gave her a big smooch on the lips!

"No! No! It's impolite to be so personal," the doctor said. "Wakko?"

"I disagree," Wakko said, gawking at the nurse.

Scratchansniff threw his hands into the air. This wasn't working at all!

"Now we will work on diction," the doctor explained. At least he might be able to teach the Animaniacs how to *speak* clearly. "How do we avoid bad elocution?"

"Stay inside during a thunderstorm," Yakko said.

"No! No! Not *electrocution*! Elocution! Diction, pronunciation!" he said in a huff. He pulled down a chart with the vowels on it. "Let's pronounce this: A-E-I-O-U."

The Animaniacs squinted up at the chart, confused. Then they read it aloud as one word: "Aaeeeiooouu."

"No! No! I want the letters!" Dr. Scratchansniff shouted.

On cue, the Animaniacs zipped into postman costumes and tossed dozens of letters his way.

"Stop! In your seats!" the doctor said. This was really getting to be too much. "If you want to go to the party, you must stop with the gags!"

In a flash, the Animaniacs put cloth
gags over their mouths. "Oh, all right,"
they said together and pulled off the gags.

Table manners were next on the list.

"Table manners are of the utmost importance," the doctor lectured. The Animaniacs were seated at a fancy dinner table in the doctor's office. "You'll eat a practice meal while I coach you along. Begin!"

The Animaniacs began to eat their food as fast as they could. Wakko ate with his hands. Yakko tossed food in the air and caught it in his mouth. Dot slurped from her soup bowl.

"Don't eat with your hands!" the doctor yelled. "You must use the proper tools!"

Scratchansniff took a deep breath and picked up a fork. "A salad fork, a dinner fork ..." He ran through all of the utensils, one at a time. "A dinner spoon, a salad knife, a bread plate," he finished, panting. "Got that?"

But the Animaniacs were playing cards. They were using dinnerware as chips to place bets.

"You're not paying attention!" the doctor shouted. "You're not listening to anything I say!"

"Sure we are," Yakko protested.

With that, the Animaniacs launched into a song, making fun of everything Scratchansniff had been trying to teach them. They paraded around the room.

"No! No!" Dr. Scratchansniff sobbed. He pounded on the desk. "I give up! You're not going to the party!"

The Animaniacs looked shocked. "Not going to the party?" they asked. "Why?"

"Why?" the doctor asked in disbelief. His face was turning red. "Why? Because you won't be polite, speak correctly, or say 'How dooo you dooo'!" he screamed in a fury.

"Oh, that," Dot said.

The Animaniacs scurried away. A second later, they appeared in formal attire.

"How dooo you dooo?" they recited politely.

Scratchansniff stared at them in surprise. "You ... you can do that?" he asked.

"Sure!" Dot replied.

The doctor gave a crooked smile. "Well then," he said. "Let's party!"

As Mr. Plotz led the investors toward the ballroom, he tried to think of something to say.

"This party is our way of saying welcome," he said. He gave them a shaky thumbs-up. "And that you're A-OK, pardner."

The investors looked at Mr. Plotz. They didn't even smile.

Mr. Plotz sighed. This wasn't going very well.

Just then Ralph approached Mr. Plotz. "Dr. Scratchansniff is arriving with the Animaniacs," he whispered.

Mr. Plotz looked toward the heavens and clasped his hands together. "Please let them behave!" he said.

"May I present," Dr. Scratchansniff said a moment later, "... the Animaniacs." Yakko and Wakko bowed, and Dot curtsied. "How dooo you dooo," they said in unison.

The investors bowed to the Animaniacs, and Yakko began to tell zany jokes. The investors who had been so stiff were now laughing like crazy.

Inside the ballroom, the Animaniacs gasped. The decorations were gorgeous. The food looked yummy. And best of all, movie stars were everywhere! Everybody who was anybody was there. This was going to be a blast!

Behind them, Mr. Plotz was congratulating Dr. Scratchansniff. "Good work," he said with a smile. "They behaved!" Then Plotz pulled the doctor close.

"Now get 'em out of here."

"But they did their part of the bargain!" Dr. Scratchansniff objected.

"I don't care," the boss said. "They're not gonna mess this up. Get 'em out!"

Dr. Scratchansniff frowned as the chairman stormed away. This was a rotten deal. He pushed the Animaniacs out a side door. "I'm sorry," he said, "but the Big Boss says you have to leave."

"But we behaved!" Dot protested.

"I know... I'm sorry," Scratchansniff said. "Now go." He turned and walked away.

"No dancing with Michelle Pfeiffer?" Yakko complained.

"No dinner with Mel Gibson?" Dot sobbed.

"No chitchat with Don Knotts?" Wakko pouted.

One after the other, the Animaniacs started to walk out.

"I know when we're not wanted," Yakko declared sadly. "I know when we

should just go home!" There was a
pause. "And now is *not* one of those
times!"

The three Animaniacs turned around
and headed straight back to the party.

Across the room, one of the investors
spotted the Animaniacs. "Look," he
said.

Mr. Plotz looked to where the
investor was pointing. "The
Animaniacs!" he said in a panic. He had
to find Scratchansniff!

A second later, he was screaming at
the doctor. "The Animaniacs are here!
You've got to help me catch them!"

Meanwhile, Wakko and Yakko were introducing themselves to the beautiful Michelle Pfeiffer.

"Who are you?" she asked.

"We're the Animaniacs!" they replied.

Mr. Plotz spotted them across the room. "There they are!" he shouted.

Yakko and Wakko jumped, then bowed to Michelle. "Save me a spot on your dance card!" Yakko said, speeding away.

They bounded up to the stage and took the place of the three musicians. Hiding behind the music stands, they fiddled a funny tune.

"Get them!" Mr. Plotz shouted.

The Animaniacs dropped their instruments . . . and ran right across the investors' dinner table! Food flew everywhere. The men were covered in chicken and sauce!

The chairman stopped in his tracks. "Oh! Those — they — I — !" he sputtered. "Arrrrrgh!" He was so angry he could barely speak.

The Animaniacs scampered up a wall and swung from a chandelier. But Mr. Plotz was right behind them. He stood on Dr. Scratchansniff's shoulders, and grabbed onto the swaying light fixture.

The cable holding the chandelier creaked under the weight, then snapped, and everyone crashed to the ground.

Mr. Plotz grabbed the Animaniacs by the scruffs of their necks. "You, you . . . you whatevers!" he screeched.

Just then he felt a tap on his shoulder. Turning around, he found himself face-to-face with the investors!

"We would like to know who is responsible for all of this," one of them said.

The chairman dropped the Animaniacs. "<u>They're</u> responsible!" he declared, pointing at them.

The investors turned to the Animaniacs and smiled. "Great party," they said. Then they handed Yakko a check for one billion dollars!

As the investors moved off, Mr. Plotz's jaw dropped. "That's my check!" he shouted.

But the Animaniacs had already disappeared, leaving Mr. Plotz in a cloud of dust.

"Gimme that!" he shouted, running after them. "That's mine! Hey...!"